MART... ...
ADVENTURES

THE
ARCTIC
QUEST

Books let your imagination soar!

minda ❀

Written and illustrated by
Minda Gomez

**For my Morenazo and my
three sweet and spicy Mexigringos:
¡Son mi bendición más grande!**

Text copyright © 2022 by Minda Gomez
Illustrations copyright ©2022 by Minda Gomez
Layout and Design by Moisés Gómez, MoGo Multimedia
Edited by Lor Calico, Calico Editing
Published by MoGo Multimedia

First paperback edition 2022   ISBN: 979-8-9853161-5-5
First hardcover edition 2022   ISBN: 979-8-9853161-6-2

Table of Contents

Values:

- **Cooperation**
- **Responsibility**
- **Perseverance**
- **Encouragement**

Meet the Martinez Family

Rico
8 years old

Diego
5 years old

Araceli
2½ years old

Papi

Mami

SPANISH WORDS

SPANISH	ENGLISH	PRONUNCIATION
Abrazos	Hugs	(ah-BRAH-sohs)
Abuelita	Grandma	(ah-bweh-LEE-tuh)
Abuelito	Grandpa	(ah-bweh-LEE-toh)
Abuelitos	Grandparents	(ah-bweh-LEE-tohs)
Ahorita regreso	I'll be right back	(ah-or-REE-tuh ree-GREH-soh)
Al fin llegaron	You finally arrived	(ahl FEEN yeh-GAHR-ohn)
Amiga	Friend (female)	(ah-MEE-guh)
Amigo	Friend (male)	(ah-MEE-goh)
Amigos	Friends	(ah-MEE-goce)
Amiguitos	Little friends	(ah-mee-GEE-toce)
Amor	My love	(ah-MOHR)
Amores	My loves	(ah-MOHR-ayce)
Atole de avena	Oatmeal drink	(uh-TOHL-eh deh ah-BEH-nah)
¡Ayúdame!	Help!	ah-YOO-dah-meh)
Bienvenido a nuestra casa	Welcome to our home	(byehn-ben-NEE-doh ah NWEHS-trah CAH-sah)
Buenas tardes	Good afternoon	(BWAY-nahs TAHR-dayce)
Caldo de pollo	Chicken soup	(CALL-doh deh POY-yoh)
Casa	House	(CAH-sah)
Chamacos	Kids	(chah-MAH-koce)
Chido	Cool	(CHEE-doh)
Chiquita	Little one	(chee-KEE-tuh)
Cinco	Five	(SEEN-koh)
Cuatro	Four	(KWAH-troh)
Diecinueve	Nineteen	(dyeh-see-NWAY-beh)
Dieguito	Little Diego	(dyeh-GEE-toh)
Discúlpame	Excuse me	(dis-CUHL-pah-meh)
Está bien	It's OK	(eh-STAH bee-YEHN)
Estados Unidos	United States	(eh-STAH-dohce yu-NEE-dohce)
¡Feliz Navidad!	Merry Christmas!	(feh-LEECE nah-bEE-dahd)
Foca	Seal	(FOH-cah)
Garita	Border checkpoint	(gah-REE-tah)

SPANISH WORDS

SPANISH	ENGLISH	PRONUNCIATION
Gracias	Thank you	(GRAH-syahce)
Hermanita	Little sister	(ehr-mah-NEE-tah)
Hermanos	Brothers	(ehr-MAH-noce)
Hijo	Son	(EE-hoh)
Hijos	Kids	(EE-hoce)
Jícamas	Mexican turnip/yam	(HEE-cah-mus)
Lentes	Glasses	(LEHN-tayce)
Listo	Ready	(LEES-tohs)
Mami	Mom	(MAH-mee)
Maravilloso	Marvelous	(mahr-ah-vee-OH-soh)
Masa	Dough	(MAH-sah)
México	Mexico	(MEH-hee-koh)
Mi amor	My love	(MEE ah-MOHR)
Mis amigos	My friends	(MEES ah-MEE-gohs)
Muchacho	Boy	(moo-CHAH-choh)
Muchas gracias	Thank you very much	(MOO-chus GRAH-syus)
Muy bien	Very good	(MWEE byehn)
Navidad	Christmas	(nah-bee-DAHD)
Nietos	Grandchildren	(nyeh-TOHS)
Nieve	Snow	(NYEH-beh)
No sé	I don't know	(no SAY)
No te preocupes	Don't worry	(NO teh preh-oh-KOO-pehs)
Nochebuena	Christmas Eve	(noh-cheh-BWEH-nah)
Paciencia	Patience	(pah-SYEHN-syah)
Piñata	Decorated figure filled with treats	(pee-NYAH-tah)
Pingüinos	Penguins	(peen-GWEE-noce)
Pollo	Chicken	(POH-yoh)
Ponche de frutas	Hot punch with fruit	(POHN-cheh deh FROO-tuhs)
Por favor	Please	(POHR fah-BOHR)
¿Qué?	What?	(KEH)
Qué rico	Delicious	(keh REE-koh)

SPANISH WORDS

SPANISH	ENGLISH	PRONUNCIATION
Rajas con queso	Pepper strips with cheese	(RAH-hus kohn KEH-soh)
Sabor	Flavor	(sah-BOHR)
Sí	Yes	(SEEN-koh)
¡Sí, se puede!	Yes, it can be done!	(SEE seh PWEH-deh)
Soy yo	It's me	(soy YOH)
Tacos de barbacoa	Tacos with shredded beef	(TAH-koce deh bar-bah-KOH-ah)
Tamales	Traditional Mexican food	(tah-MAHL-ayce)
Tita	Nickname for Grandma	(TEE-tuh)
Tito	Nickname for Grandpa	(TEE-toh)
Todo bien	Everything is OK	(TOH-doh BYEHN)
Tortillas de harina	Flour tortillas	(tor-TEE-us DAY a-REE-nah)
Uno, dos, tres	One, two, three	(OO-noh DOHS TREHS)
Veinte	Twenty	(BEHN-teh)
Villancicos	Christmas carols	(bee-yahn-SEE-kohs)
¡Ya voy!	Coming!	(YAH VOY)

NAMES

Name	Pronunciation
Martinez	mar-TEE-nes
Rico	REE-koh
Diego	dee-AY-goh
Araceli	ah-rah-SELL-ee
Mami	MAH-mee
Papi	PAH-pee
Doña Rosa	DOHN-yah ROH-sah
Don Toño	DOHN TOHN-yo
Tito	TEE-toh
Tita	TEE-ta

Part
1
THE JOURNEY SOUTH

Alaska

The Arctic

Canada

Minnesota

Martinez home

United States

Rest Stop

Texas

and the
Coahuila

Mexico

Chapter 1
Back Again

The sun beat down in the sky as Diego swung through the leafy jungle. Extending his tail above him, the spider monkey grasped a tree branch and moved expertly ahead, high above the ground. Reaching out his long arms, he grabbed hold of a hanging vine and launched himself forward, yodeling in a loud voice.

Suddenly, Diego's vine disappeared and he briefly hung mid-air like a cartoon character. He caught his breath. This wasn't supposed to happen! Then, just as quickly, he was falling, down, down, faster and faster. "Don Toño!" he tried to yell as he tumbled downward.

A sparkling blue ocean appeared below him and

1

he splashed through the surface of the water. Diego looked around and discovered he was in a coral reef, surrounded by fish of every color of the rainbow. His strong tail propelled him forward easily.

"Am I an orca now?" he asked himself happily. Almost without thinking, he flipped his fins and leaped from the water, executing a perfect spin before gracefully diving back in. All of the smaller fish around him watched the shiny black-and-white whale in awe, admiring his skilled acrobatics.

"Diego!" The orca heard a loud voice nearby that could not have come from a tiny fish.

"Who's there?" Diego called. He swam in a circle, trying to identify where it had come from.

"Come on! Let's go play!" the voice spoke more urgently. This time Diego recognized it as his brother's voice.

"Rico? Are you a whale shark again? Where are you hiding?" he called into the crystalline water, confused that he could not determine where the enormous animal could be.

"What? A whale shark?" laughed the voice.

Diego felt something pushing him roughly in the fin.

He was suddenly aware that he was tangled in the blankets on his bed. He pried open his eyes to see his older brother Rico, still in his pajamas, his short brown hair sticking in all directions on his head.

"Diego, it snowed last night!" said his brother excitedly. "Let's go play outside!"

Sighing, Diego pulled himself out of bed and stumbled to the door. "I wish it wasn't just a dream!" he said wistfully. "When are we going to go through Don Toño's virtual reality door again?"

Chapter 2
The Snowy Day

It was a crisp winter day in Minnesota. The sun sparkled like diamonds off the snowdrifts in the backyard of the Martinez *casa*, making it hard to see without squinting. Rico, Diego, and Araceli Martinez were busy playing outside after a heavy snowfall the night before.

"Look out below!" shouted eight-year-old Rico as he catapulted down the small backyard hill on his sled. Five-year-old Diego dodged out of the way as his brother flew past him and crashed at the bottom, landing face-down in the snow.

When Rico lifted his head, his eyelashes were coated in snowflakes and his cheeks were glistening wet.

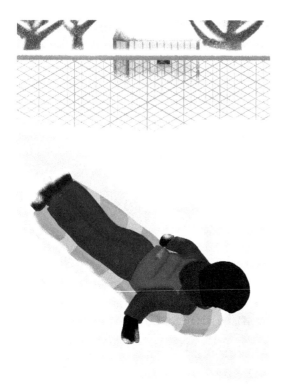

He glanced back at Diego, who was studying him to see his reaction, then burst out laughing. "That was *chido!*" he exclaimed excitedly, using his favorite Spanish word for "cool."

Diego, relieved to see that his brother was OK, laughed along with Rico as he began to climb the hill for the next sled run.

"Hey, Diego, let's have a snowball fight!" suggested Rico.

Diego turned around just in time for an icy ball to smash into his face. He spit snow out of his mouth. "Rico! I wasn't ready!" he shouted. He lunged at the bigger boy and tried to tackle him. Rico lost his balance and toppled over. The two boys began to wrestle in the soft powder. Their frustration soon turned to laughter as the brothers rolled around together on the soft ground.

"¡Ayúdame! Help! So cold!" Araceli interrupted their wrestling match from where she stood a few feet away. The poor two-year-old couldn't move, encumbered by her pink winter coat, snow pants, and heavy boots hidden in knee-deep snow. She tried to take a step forward and toppled over, raising her white-powdered face to wail.

Rico and Diego glanced at each other in dismay. "Why do we always have to take care of Araceli?" asked Diego. "Little kids are no fun."

Rico agreed. "You go get her. I got her last time!" he urged. He turned to run to the other end of the backyard, leaving Diego with their crying sister.

Diego sighed, heading over to help his sister up. Gently, he brushed the snow and freezing teardrops from her face. Araceli cried for a moment longer, then stopped as Diego reached out his hand. Her brother carefully helped her walk up the steps to the deck and into the house. "It's freezing out here, isn't it?" he remarked. "Maybe Mami can make us some hot chocolate."

As he was heading back down, Diego noticed his next-door neighbor Don Toño walking toward the chain-link fence that separated their backyards. Diego looked longingly at the snow-covered shed in his neighbor's yard, remembering the previous summer.

For as normal as the friendly Mexican man seemed, he was actually a brilliant inventor, and the ordinary garden shed was in fact a virtual reality machine that could transform the kids into animals and send them to exotic places. Diego hadn't stopped dreaming of the incredible world that lay behind the secret door. He was eager to step through it again.

Recently, though, the shed had been closed up, and the kids hadn't seen much of Don Toño and his wife Doña Rosa. Everyone in Minnesota had a tendency to hibernate in the wintertime.

Diego trudged over to greet his neighbor at the fence. The elderly Mexican man's gray hair was covered by a multicolored stocking cap, hand-knit by Doña Rosa. His gray bushy eyebrows waggled as he smiled at Diego over the fence. *"Buenas tardes, amiguito!"* the old man greeted him affectionately. "Are you having fun in the snow?"

"It's OK," replied Diego indifferently. "I'm tired of playing with Araceli and Rico. All of my friends are at the sledding hill today, but Mami and Papi said that we have to stay home so they can pack for our trip to Mexico."

"¿Qué?" questioned Don Toño, showing his surprise. "When did you decide to go to *México?*"

Diego scrunched up his nose. "Mami and Papi decided we're going to DRIVE down to Mexico for Christmas with Tita and Tito. I'm going to be stuck in the van for three whole days!"

Don Toño smiled approvingly at the boy. "I'm sure your *abuelos* will be thrilled to spend *Navidad* with you. You kids are their youngest grandchildren."

"Yeah, I love my grandparents… but I will miss celebrating Christmas here in Minnesota like we usually do. Christmas is supposed to be snowy, and Tita and Tito are so… old," Diego confessed.

Don Toño stood looking down at his young friend with a thoughtful look on his face. *"Ahorita regreso. I'll be right back."* He turned to walk slowly in the direction of the garden shed. Diego held his breath. Might Don Toño be inviting them to have another adventure? The old man pulled on the door and entered the shed.

When he emerged a minute later, he was holding a package the size of a shoebox, wrapped in shiny foil paper and tied with a sparkly bow. The gift caught Rico's eye, and he ran up to join Diego at the fence.

"What's in the box, Don Toño?" called Rico. "Is that for me?"

"No, it's for me!" argued Diego. "He was talking to ME."

"No fair!" whined Rico, feeling his eyes start to fill up with tears. "You ALWAYS get the special treatment because you're younger than me! Being the oldest is

no fun!"

"That's not true!" retorted Diego. "You think just because you're the oldest, YOU should get everything first." This was clearly not the first time they had argued over this.

Their argument was cut short as Don Toño finished his slow walk up to the fence with the box in his gloved hands. The old man cleared his throat, waiting for the boys to stop arguing. The boys looked expectantly at their neighbor and the gift.

"I have been working on a new project and could use some help with it. Do you think there's any way you could find a moment to give me a hand?"

Diego's face brightened. The last time Don Toño had asked them for help, they had turned into squirrels, whales, sharks, and monkeys. What kind of surprise did Don Toño have up his sleeve this time? "I can help you, Don Toño," he offered helpfully.

Rico pouted. "What about me? Where's my present?"

Don Toño looked from one boy to the other and twitched his white mustache thoughtfully. "I actually need all three of you *chamacos* to try it out together and tell me what you think," he said. He handed the box over the fence to Diego.

"Gracias," both boys thanked their neighbor excitedly, beginning to pull their gloves off to rip open the package.

Don Toño stopped them. "Hold on! I do have one very important condition. Promise me that you will let your *mami* hold onto the box until you get to Texas."

"How far is Texas?" Diego asked.

"It'll take about two days to get there." Rico frowned.

Diego looked surprised. "I don't think I can wait that long!" he whined. "Our drive is going to be SO boring!"

"I don't know about that," said Don Toño with a mysterious smile on his face. *"¡Buen viaje!* Have a great trip!"

Chapter 3
The Gift

"Can we open it NOW?" came a voice from the back of the minivan. It was the final day of the journey from Minnesota to the Mexican border town where Papi's parents lived. The family was driving through a sea of yellow Texas fields of long grass.

Mami turned around from the front passenger seat. "No, not yet. It's not a good time," she explained, brushing a strand of long blonde hair behind her ear with her hand.

Three children groaned from the back. "We'll be stopping for a break soon. Why don't you kids do some mazes or read a book?" she suggested.

"We already did that!" returned Rico, forgetting his parents' earlier lecture about having a positive attitude. "I'm tired of being in the van."

"Me too!" complained Diego. "This van is TOO crowded, and I'm sick of being so close to Rico."

Mami turned around to see her children. "Don Toño said that the three of you need to open the gift together. How is that going to work if you're fighting?"

"We won't fight anymore," promised Rico quickly. "Can I open it? I'm the oldest so I should get to see it first."

"ME open it!" exclaimed Araceli. "It MINE!"

"What about me?" asked Diego, realizing he would have to stick up for himself. "Don Toño gave it to ME!"

The three children began arguing once again.

"Let's make a deal," suggested Mami, consulting the GPS map on her phone. "The next rest stop is coming up in about 15 minutes. If you kids can go that distance without fighting or complaining, we will open it up there."

"Fifteen minutes! That's almost the same as FOREVER!" said Diego impatiently, but after a warning glance from Mami, he closed his mouth. The following moments seemed to take a lifetime, but the kids managed to ride peacefully. Even Rico and Diego had to admit that the silence helped them to relax a bit.

Papi finally pulled off on the exit and the family climbed out of the van. The warm winter weather in Texas was different from the icy cold of Minnesota. The kids enjoyed the feeling of the sun on their faces as they gathered around Mami with the box at a picnic table.

Together, the three Martinez kids pulled the sparkly ribbon to loosen it, ripped off the paper, and with expectation, lifted the cover from the shoebox. A groan exited Rico's mouth as he caught a glimpse. "This is IT? Plastic sunglasses?" he grumbled with disappointment. "I expected more out of Don Toño."

"Me like pink *lentes!*" proclaimed Araceli, reaching

to grab a pair of plastic glasses and slip them on her face. She instantly let out a shriek. "What happening?!" she shouted in her little voice. "It so cold! Why there *nieve?*" She yanked the glasses from her face and a look of confused relief came over her. She handed the glasses to Mami. "Too scary."

Rico and Diego observed their little sister with a combination of concern and fascination. What could have just happened with the plastic sunglasses to make their brave little sister react that way?

The boys looked at each other, then cautiously started to reach into the box for the glasses. It couldn't be THAT scary if Don Toño sent them, could it?

Right then, Papi came out of the rest area building and approached the group, quickly swiping the box from the table and holding it out of the boys' reach. "I forgot to tell you. Don Toño told me to make sure we read the note before we touch anything."

The boys protested but sat obediently as Mami reached into the box to pull out a small sheet of paper. "Here it is, kids. Let's see what this note says."

 She began to read aloud:

"Mis amigos, I found a way to use the technology from the shed to create a portable version of my virtual reality transporter. Put on the glasses, and the fun will begin. Just make sure not to use them when you are standing up... you might run into something! ¡Feliz Navidad!"

"Chido!" exclaimed Rico and Diego at the same time. "Can we have them now?" they begged Papi.

"Slow down, *chicos.* We need to get back on the road. How about you try them out in the van?" suggested Papi. The boys raced to the doors and jumped into their seats, quickly buckling themselves in.

As Papi pulled the van back onto the freeway, Mami turned around in her seat to look at her three kids.

"OK, from what I can gather, these sunglasses are really virtual reality glasses. In real life, you will still be here in the van with us, but you will feel like you are wherever Don Toño programmed them to take you. If you need to come back, just reach up and pull off the glasses. Can you look out for Araceli?"

"Yes, Mami," the boys promised.

"No scary," stated Araceli, putting on a brave face. "Me big girl." She glanced at her brothers for reassurance that they would be with her.

"Hey, Mami, do you know where we're going this time? Or what animal we're going to turn into?"

questioned Diego.

"The note doesn't say. But if I know Don Toño, he has a reason for wherever he plans to send you." Mami handed a pair of glasses to each child. "OK, on the count of three, put on your glasses!"

Buckled into their seats, Rico, Diego, and Araceli held their glasses up as Mami counted. *"Uno, dos, TRES!"*

As they placed the plastic frames on their faces, the van began to spin around them. "Wooooooooah!" screamed the three Martinez kids in unison, feeling themselves being swept out of their seats and set down on solid ground. They were blinded by a bright light, and an icy blast hit them sharply. Where had they been taken?

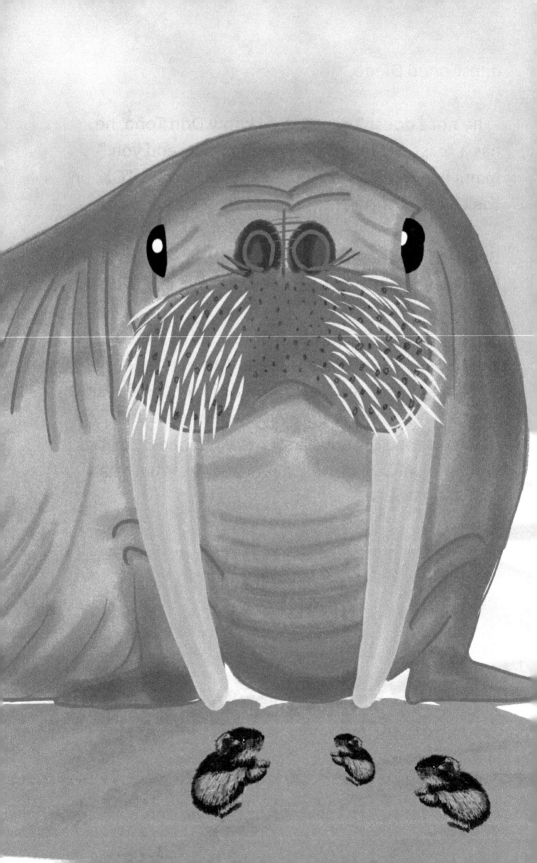

Chapter 4
Into the Arctic

"Woooah! What a ride!" marveled Rico. "I'll never get used to the swirling as we move into Don Toño's worlds."

"Where did the van go?" wondered Diego. "How did Don Toño do this?"

As Rico, Diego, and Araceli's eyes adjusted to the bright light, they looked around. Everything was white, stretching flat out around them in all directions. Jagged snow-covered mountains jutted up in the distance on one side. In the other direction, a few skinny pine trees protruded out of the otherwise smooth landscape. Directly above them, the sun shone brightly against a brilliant blue sky, but it didn't seem to provide any warmth. The three huddled into a little group on the ice, trying to keep warm.

"So cold! Brrrr!" exclaimed Araceli.

"Where are we?" Rico shivered. "This is NOT the rainforest."

"Or the coral reef!" agreed Diego. "It's FREEZING here! I wonder where we are?"

"You are in the Arctic Circle," came a booming voice from above them. The Martinez kids separated from their huddle to look up, startled to see an enormous brown walrus towering over them. Whiskers hung down from his large, rounded snout, and long ivory tusks curved down, seeming to point straight at them.

All three kids screamed in terror.

"Run! It's a giant monster!" shouted Rico, turning to scamper across the ice.

"Chamacos, soy yo. It's me, Don Toño." The kids now recognized the familiar voice of their neighbor coming from the walrus.

"Don Toño! You're huge! How did you get here? We're in the van on the way to Mexico right now!" asked Rico incredulously. "Or I mean, we WERE in the van... we're still there in real life, right?"

"Yes," chuckled the walrus, lowering his immense head to the icy ground to look them over. "This is just virtual reality. The beauty of technology is that it allows us to be together even when we're not physically in the same place. Kind of like when you talk to your family in Mexico on video chat."

"*Chido!*" marveled Diego. He finally tore his gaze away from the giant walrus and looked over at his brother and sister, still shivering next to him on the ice. Small, furry black and brown bodies shaped like little mice with stubby tails looked back at him with their beady black eyes. He glanced down to see that he was covered with the same fur. "We're kind of funny-looking! What are we?" he asked.

"Lemmings!" concluded Rico. "I've seen them on TV. They're really funny, and like to jump off the side of cliffs. Wait... do we need to do that?"

"Actually," corrected Don Toño, "that's just a myth,

but they do know how to swim, and sometimes groups of lemmings jump into the water to move to a new place when their population grows too big."

"How do you say lemming in Spanish?" wondered Diego. "I don't think I've learned that word in kindergarten." He took pride in the new words he was learning at the Spanish immersion school he attended.

"Lemming," Don Toño pronounced with a Spanish flair. "Basically the same as English."

"Cool!" said Diego, watching his little sister scamper around in the snow. "We're so CUTE!" He ran after Araceli and playfully tackled her. She squealed with delight.

Rico ran up on his stubby little legs and jumped into a pile of snow nearby, showering the air with a light powder that drifted gently down on their fluffy heads. The icy temperature wasn't bothering them anymore… it was as if their bodies were made to tolerate the cold.

"This is really fun!" observed Rico. "I'm glad we can

still play in the snow! This fur is better than my
warmest coat and boots."

"That's right," chuckled Don Toño. "I know you
were worried about not having a white Christmas. I
decided to bring the snow to you!"

The walrus paused for a moment as if he were
listening to a silent voice. *"Ya voy, mi amorcito!*
Coming, my love!" he called into the air. He looked at
his young friends. "Doña Rosa is calling me for lunch.
I'll be back to check on you in a little while. Have fun,
my little lemmings!" With a poof, the giant walrus
vanished into thin air, leaving the three lemmings

staring at where he had been.

Araceli screamed. "Where he go?" She turned to her brothers to make sure they were still with her. "You stay here, OK?"

"Don Toño will be back later," explained Diego. "Rico and I aren't going to leave you. We'll stay right here with you." He glanced over at Rico to see if his older brother was also going to keep his promise to help look after Araceli. His brother didn't appear to be listening.

"Look! Let's make a snowman!" suggested Rico. He pushed with all his might to create a ball of snow. "This is probably only the size of a golf ball, but it feels huge!"

Diego worked to create a second ball and pushed it over to where Rico had set the first one. "I can't get it up there by myself! Can you help me?" His brother scurried over and used his tiny paws to help Diego lift the ball on top of the bottom part of the snowman.

"Who help me?" questioned Araceli, struggling to

gather the snow into a ball.

"You help her!" said Rico to Diego. "I'm going to go play!" He darted away, leaving his brother alone with Araceli.

"Rico!" whined Diego as he moved over to his sister and helped her to create a tiny snowball. They tried their best, but were unable to lift the ball on top of the other two.

"Rico, can you PLEASE help us? We need you!" called Diego.

Reluctantly, Rico came back, and the three lemmings lifted the final ball onto the stack, creating a snowman that stood as tall as they were.

Diego stood admiring their handiwork. "Now we just need a mini carrot for his nose and a tiny scarf to go around his neck."

"It turned out really cute!" admitted Rico.

Just then, with a poof, the giant walrus appeared next to them again.

"Aaah!" they shouted, startled.

"You scared me, Don Toño!" Rico accused his neighbor playfully.

"Discúlpame," apologized Don Toño. "I was enjoying the memory of the delicious *caldo de pollo* that Doña Rosa made for me."

"Chicken soup? Yum! I'm starting to feel kind of hungry," admitted Diego. "Can we have a snack?"

"If you can find some leaves or bark to eat, help yourself," said Don Toño. "That's lemming food. Otherwise, you might need to wait for lunchtime. But first, I do have another favor to ask." There was a glint in his eyes as he looked at the tiny lemmings over his mustached snout and tusks. "I know you are having fun as lemmings, but I need to do some more research. Does anybody want to try out another animal avatar?"

"Meeeee!" shouted all three little lemmings at once, bouncing up and down on their stubby legs.

Chapter 5
The Challenge

The lemmings looked up excitedly at Don Toño the walrus.

"How do we change to another animal?" asked Diego. "Can we do it right now? I want to be a penguin!"

"Sorry to break it to you, but *pingüinos* only live in Antarctica... the South Pole. We are near the North Pole," corrected Don Toño, now speaking in his teacher voice.

"This is interesting and all, but how does it work?" urged Rico impatiently.

"*Paciencia, muchacho.* Patience, my boy," murmured Don Toño, his tiny eyes peering through the heavy wrinkles of his head. "Before you change animals, I have prepared a challenge that you need to complete. Solving the challenge will lead you to the key to your transformation. I'm sure it will be easy for you. All you need to do is read the clue."

"What clue? How do we find it?" questioned Diego. "We're so little!"

The gigantic pinniped looked down at the tiny rodents with a knowing smile. "If you climb up to the top of that snowbank, you should be able to see the clue! I think you will figure it out between the three of you." The walrus paused and looked at his friends and continued. "I'm working to incorporate each of the five senses to make the experience more realistic. Can you each choose a different animal and report back to me?"

"Yes, Don Toño," responded the three together.

"Maravilloso!" Don Toño's eyes twinkled. "I will get the full report when you are home. Now, if you'll excuse me, *amiguitos*, I'm going to go for a swim to cool down. This blubber is insulating a little too well and I'm feeling rather warm."

He twitched his mustache, then began to heft his giant, wobbly body along the ice, using his flippers to move. Eventually, he pulled himself to the edge of the ice and looked back."Don't forget to work together! *¡Feliz Navidad!"* He flopped into the water and dipped below the surface.

"This is so exciting!" exclaimed Diego. "I feel like a real scientist, helping Don Toño out this way."

"What are we waiting for? Let's go find the clue!" shouted Rico.

"Me no want that!" declared Araceli, squeaking in her tiny little voice and laughing. "Me play self!" She did a log roll in the snow, giggling in her melodious little voice.

"I bet I can find it before you do! First one to find it wins!" Rico challenged Diego. He raced toward a snowbank and tried to climb it, surprised to feel himself sinking down into the fluffy snow.

"No fair!" whined Diego. "I wasn't ready." He followed behind his brother and soon found himself buried to the tip of his tiny nose. Shaking his furry body to free himself, Diego emerged to see Rico laughing.

"Hey, don't tease me! You couldn't do it either." Diego started to giggle, thinking how funny he must look. "This is going to be harder than we thought!" He paused to think. "Remember, Don Toño told us we have to work together. How can we get up high enough to look for a clue?" He looked around, realizing that each small mound of snow was like a mountain to a lemming.

"Look over here!" shouted Rico from a distance

away. "Araceli found something cool!" On the other side of a snowbank was a rock that appeared as big as a mountain to the tiny lemmings. "I bet if we climb up there, we will be able to see the clue." He scurried over and attempted to climb up the rock, but found himself slipping down again. "It's icy… I can't get up!"

"Me do it self!" declared Araceli, taking a running leap and jumping as high as she could toward the rock. Unable to get her grip on the icy surface, the tiniest lemming slid down the rock, with a frustrated expression on her face.

"I'll show you how it's done!" said Diego, scampering through the white powder to the rock. For a second, he thought he would be able to scale the rock, but soon found his little feet slipping. The next thing he knew, he was on his back looking up at the giant rock. "How can we work together?" he asked himself thoughtfully. "I know! What if we make a lemming tower, like a snowman?"

"Good idea, Diego! Wow, for a five-year-old, you're really smart!" affirmed Rico encouragingly.

"I'm almost six!" Diego reminded him. "Rico, you're the biggest. Can you be on the bottom?" He gestured to where he wanted his brother to stand.

"Sure," agreed Rico. He stood on his hind legs, propping his front paws against the rock.

Diego climbed up his brother's soft back and drew himself to a standing position on Rico's shoulders. "Araceli, you're the littlest. Can you climb up on my back?"

Araceli scrambled easily up her brothers and stood on Diego's shoulders. "Snowman!" she exclaimed. She made a leap onto the top of the rock and scanned the area. "Me see it! There!" She pointed with her tiny paw in the opposite direction from where the boys had been looking. "What it say?" she questioned, twitching her whiskers quickly.

"I can't see from here. Can you lift us up?" asked

Diego hopefully.

"No. You big!" stated Araceli, peering down over the side of the rock.

"That's OK, Araceli! You can come down now," said Rico. "Wow, I can't believe she found it!" After helping Araceli climb back down from the rock, the three little lemmings scurried in the direction Araceli had pointed. As they got closer, they could see a message written in a snowdrift.

TOUCH THE STONE
TO CHOOSE YOUR ANIMAL

An arrow pointed to an area where the snow had been cleared away from the icy ground. On the ice was an arrangement of statues that appeared to be carved out of rock. Each statue stood a bit taller than a lemming. They scurried over to examine them.

"Animals!" exclaimed Araceli.
Sure enough, the stones were carved into the shape of a polar bear, a snowy owl, and a harp seal. "Wait, so if we touch them we turn into this animal?"

questioned Diego.

"Remember, Don Toño said we each have to be a different animal so we can report back afterwards," Rico reminded them.

"Yay!" cheered Araceli, racing toward the statues. "Me like *foca!*" Before her brothers could stop her, she reached out to touch the statue of the harp seal.

Instantly, an incredible transformation began. Her brown and black fur began to glow and, starting at her stubby tail, her body began to turn white. The color worked its way up her body until she was white from head to tail. Then, her tiny body began to change shape, expanding like a balloon until she was about two feet long. She flopped on the ice, an adorable baby seal with a face that resembled a puppy dog.

Diego and Rico, still little lemmings, stared up at their little sister, who was now much bigger than they were. "Awww, she's sooooo cute!" exclaimed Diego.

Rico sat back, admiring Araceli. "She's beautiful!"

"Yeah, me cute! Me princess *foca*," decided Araceli.

She rolled over and giggled. It was clear she was having a wonderful time. She paused to stare down at the two lemmings. "Why you small?"

This snapped the brothers out of it. They turned to glance at each other, then both turned toward the statues at the same time. "I want to be the owl so I can fly!" shouted Diego. He started to reach toward the owl statue but was tackled by Rico's fluffy body.

"Not so fast! I want to fly too!" Rico and Diego began to roll around in the snow, wrestling and definitely not laughing this time.

"Come on! You always get what you want!" argued Diego.

"Not true! But I AM the oldest, so I should get to do it first." Rico scurried toward the statues and began

to reach for the owl as Diego opened his whiskered mouth to protest again.

At that moment, Araceli silently vanished before their eyes. The two lemmings stopped fighting to look at each other.

"Oh no! Where'd she go?" questioned Diego, looking concerned. "Do you think she's OK?"

Rico glanced around the snowy landscape quickly, anxious to have his chance. "I hope so! She'll be fine." Just as he reached out his paw to touch the owl statue, he too disappeared as if he had evaporated into the frigid air.

A concerned Diego remained, standing alone and swinging his tiny head to check around him. "Rico? Araceli?" He couldn't find his siblings anywhere! Would he be left here all alone? Did he even remember how to go back?

"Don Toño?" he called in a worried voice. "Are you here?" But all was silent, except for the whistle of the Arctic wind blowing past.

Chapter 6
Tita and Tito

At that moment, the Arctic scene began to swirl around Diego. A second later, he found himself strapped into his seat in the van. Papi was standing by the open sliding door, holding three folded pairs of plastic sunglasses in his hand. "Sorry to take your glasses off, *hijo*. It sounded like you were having fun. We've arrived in *México*," Papi explained.

Diego protested. "No fair! I never even got to be another animal!"

"Enough!" Papi cut Diego's complaint short. "We're here now, and it's time to enjoy this time with family. Let's go say hi to your grandparents. Rico and Araceli are already inside."

Diego unbuckled himself from his seat and hopped out of the van. He stopped to stretch his legs before he followed Papi up the sidewalk and into the small, brightly-painted house owned by his grandparents. Papi's mother Tita, short for *abuelita*, stood in the doorway.

"Dieguito, *mi amor,*" said Tita to Diego as she greeted him with a big hug and a kiss on the cheek. *"¡Feliz Navidad! Bienvenido a nuestra casa."*

"Merry Christmas. Welcome to our house," Diego translated in his head. *"Gracias,* Tita," he responded, thinking how his Spanish was going to get a workout during this trip.

Walking up behind Tita came Tito, Papi's father. *"¡Al fin llegaron!"* he said contentedly as he hugged his grandson.

"You finally arrived," Diego translated to himself as Tito greeted them with hugs and kisses on the cheek.

Diego temporarily forgot about the drama in the Arctic as he settled into his grandparents' house.

Tita ushered them into the kitchen where she had mugs of steaming *atole de avena* waiting for them. The kids thirstily slurped the sweet oatmeal drink made with condensed milk and cinnamon sticks.

"This is delicious!" Diego announced. "I mean, *¡qué rico!*" he clarified, looking at Tita with a smile. Rico and Araceli agreed, licking their lips happily.

Later that afternoon, Mami took Araceli to the bedroom for her nap. Rico and Diego ran up to Papi. "Can we use the glasses again? Pleeeease?" they begged, staring up at Papi with their big, brown puppy dog eyes.

Papi looked down at his two sons. "No, *hijos,* we aren't going to use the glasses while we're here in Mexico. This week is about spending time with your *abuelos* and being together as a family. Why don't you two go and play outside for a while?"

Knowing Papi wasn't going to change his mind, the boys headed outside to play in the front yard, which was surrounded by a tall iron fence with a gate. As they kicked a soccer ball back and forth on the dry grass, Rico spoke up. "I wish you would have let me pick the owl."

Diego looked back at Rico with a serious look on his face. "I just feel sad we let Don Toño down. He wanted us to check out the different animals, but we didn't even get to try them out."

"That's true," admitted Rico. "We wasted a lot of time fighting. Let's try to get along better next time... Do you think we'll be able to have another chance?"

"I hope so," Diego replied.
During the days that followed, Tita filled the kids' stomachs with delicious Mexican treats and

traditional cooking. Almost every day, Tita made a batch of her famous *tortillas de harina,* and each time, she chose a grandchild to help her make them. Diego was excited to show her that he had learned how to roll out the tortillas from his neighbor in Minnesota, Doña Rosa. "I think you two would get along really well," he commented wisely.

Every morning, Tito and Papi headed out to go for walks through town. One morning, they brought back *tacos de barbacoa* to eat for breakfast, along with a delicious spicy salsa that came tied up in a plastic bag.

Other mornings, Tita served scrambled eggs with spicy *chorizo* sausage, along with flavorful beans from the slow cooker. Everything was, of course, accompanied by tortillas.

The day before Christmas Eve, the whole family set up an assembly line making *tamales.* Tita taught them to begin by putting down a corn husk on the table. They spread it with *masa* – dough made from corn flour. Then, they added a layer of filling to the middle. There was pork with red salsa, chicken with green salsa, and *rajas con queso* – strips of peppers with cheese. They even made some *tamales* with raisins, cinnamon, and sweet *masa*. After wrapping the *tamales* up in the corn husks, they set them in a pot above boiling water to steam.

The Martinez kids devoured all of the food placed before them. "Mami, why doesn't your cooking taste this good?" questioned Rico at one point.

Mami looked at Rico and shrugged her shoulders. "I guess I'm still missing the authentic Mexican *sabor*," she said. "Capturing the true flavor of Mexico is a lot more than just following a recipe." She smiled at Tita fondly.

One afternoon, while Araceli was taking her nap, Tita, Tito, and the boys sat down to play a game. Playing word games in Spanish was tricky, but Diego was proud to spell some words that he was learning at school. He realized he hadn't even thought about Minnesota or the Arctic for a couple of days. "Mexico is so fun!" he said to himself. "Tito and Tita aren't boring at all!"

Chapter 7
Nochebuena

It was the morning of *Nochebuena*, the Spanish word for Christmas Eve. Papi had explained to the kids that in Mexico, Christmas is celebrated on the night of December 24. "I'm so excited for Christmas!" cheered Diego happily.

Tita was working to prepare *ponche de frutas*, a hot fruit drink with chunks of apple and guava floating in it, flavored with cinnamon sticks and sugar cane. She gave Araceli a sample to taste.

"Mmmm!" Araceli announced. "Me like *ponche.*"

A while later, Mami spoke with Rico and Diego. "Would you kids help with Araceli tonight?" she asked. "I'm going to be helping Tita with the food, and I'm sure Papi will be busy enjoying time with his family. It would mean a lot."

The brothers hesitated, looked at each other, and nodded.

"Sure, Mami, we can watch her," Rico responded.

"We can take turns," added Diego. "I just hope we can still have fun with her around."

When evening came, aunts, uncles, and cousins started to arrive at Tita and Tito's house. Everybody greeted each other with hugs and kisses. As the family sat around tables on folding chairs, enjoying their mouth-watering *tamale* feast, sounds of laughter filled the air.

Rico, Diego, and Araceli were pleasantly surprised that they were allowed to stay up past their bedtime that night. They cheered when Tito came walking out with a *piñata* and hung it up in the tree outside the house. From the youngest to the oldest, each of the cousins took turns being blindfolded and hitting it with a stick while everyone sang:

Dale, dale, dale, no pierdas el tino,
Porque si lo pierdes, pierdes el camino.
Ya le diste una, ya le diste dos,
¡Ya le diste tres y tu tiempo se acabó!

When the *piñata* broke open, mandarin oranges, sugar cane, peanuts, and spicy Mexican candies fell to the ground. The Martinez kids laughed gleefully as they ran around to gather up the goodies with their older cousins. Rico and Diego took extra care of Araceli and made sure she got her share of treats.

Later, the family sat in a circle around the living room and sang *villancicos* – Christmas carols. Rico and Diego sang along in English to the tunes they recognized, since they didn't know the Spanish words. Araceli twirled contentedly in the middle of the circle until she got dizzy and moved to squeeze between Rico and Diego on the couch.

When midnight arrived and it was officially Christmas Day, Diego and Rico stood up to move from person to person, receiving warm hugs and responding with: *"¡Feliz Navidad!"* By now, Araceli was stretched out on the couch, sound asleep, seemingly unbothered by the festivities around her.

Outside the house, the sound of fireworks began. The boys ran to the door to see their older cousins shooting off small fireworks from the middle of the quiet street. "Can we go too?" they pleaded to their parents.

Mami began to say no, but Papi looked at her. "This is a part of our tradition," he explained. "I'll make sure they don't get too close."

After the fireworks, the family gift exchange began. Rico and Diego sat in the living room with the rest of the family. Their eyes were drooping with sleepiness, but they were excited to see what they were going to receive. As they opened their gifts, the boys made sure they remembered to say *gracias* to the family members who had given them.

"Wow," remarked Diego. "This has been such a great Christmas! It hasn't been boring at all. We're so lucky to have family in Minnesota AND Mexico."

"Yeah," agreed Rico. "I wasn't sure I wanted to miss out on playing with my friends in Minnesota, but I haven't even missed them."

"I feel extra lucky because I get to hang out with you," said Diego to Rico shyly. "You're my best friend."

Rico smiled back at Diego and gave him a hug. "We really can have a good time together when we're

not fighting, can't we?"

A little later, Mami walked up to the boys with a box wrapped in shiny paper, similar to the one from Don Toño they had opened a few days earlier. "Kids, do either of you know where this gift came from? I found it under the tree, addressed to the three of you, but it doesn't say who it's from."

Rico and Diego looked at each other, shrugged, and looked back at Mami. "I don't know, but can we open it?" asked Rico. Mami gave it to the boys and sat down to watch.

Rico pulled the bow off and Diego ripped open the paper. Inside was a shoebox, similar to the one that had held their glasses. As Diego opened the box, both boys leaned forward excitedly to see what was inside.

By now they recognized Don Toño's handwriting in the note that sat on top of a pile of tissue paper in the box:

I thought you might want to hold onto these for your trip back.

Both boys hurried to pull aside the tissue paper. Inside the box, nestled in the paper, were three five-inch stone figurines in the shapes of different animals. The boys looked closely and realized at the same time that they were the same statues they had seen in the Arctic when they were lemmings... but they had seemed a lot bigger at the time.

Diego and Rico looked at each other. "Do you know what this means?" exclaimed Rico with an excited look on his face. "There's still a chance to go back to the Arctic! Thank you, Don Toño!" he shouted, even though he knew his neighbor couldn't hear him in Minnesota.

"Yaaaay!" cheered Diego. "More adventures to come! This has been the best Christmas ever!"

Part
2
THE JOURNEY
NORTH

Chapter 8
Adiós México

Diego waved through the window at Tita and Tito
as the van pulled away from the colorful pink house
and began its short trip through the Mexican border
town where his grandparents lived. He watched as
they passed by buildings with Spanish words painted
in large letters on the concrete walls. It wasn't the
bustling town that it had been in its heyday, but Diego
had enjoyed experiencing life in this part of Mexico.

The van drew up to the international bridge,
stretching across the Río Grande River to the United
States.

"Mami, when can we use the glasses?" Diego asked.
Mami was talking to Papi as they looked at the long

line of vehicles waiting to cross over the border from Mexico into Texas. "Mami! Are you listening to me?"

Mami looked back at him over her shoulder. *"Amor,* I need you to be patient. Let's wait until we are through the *garita."* She gestured far ahead, up the row of cars, at the tiny building on the side of the road. An official was speaking with the people in each car about their visit as they prepared to drive over to the U.S. side of the river. Papi slowly drove the van ahead a few feet and stopped again, impatiently looking at the clock on the van's dashboard. This border crossing was going to take longer than they had planned.

Rico looked up from the book he was reading. "I know it's hard to wait, Diego, but you need to be patient." His big brother put on a mature face and went back to his book. Araceli industriously drew large, bold pink and purple circles in a notebook. Diego sighed. Why was he the only one in his family who understood the urgency to go back to Don Toño's adventure?

As they waited, Mami handed each of the kids a small package of candy. Diego popped an orange bear into his mouth. "What do you call a gummy bear in Spanish?" he asked, chewing the gooey, sweet treat.

"*¡No sé!*" responded Araceli, stuffing three gummy bears into her mouth at the same time.

"Yeah, I don't know either," called Mami from the front seat. "What's the answer?"

"A *delici-OSO!*" announced Diego triumphantly, waiting for the laughter. "Get it? A delicious bear!" A few polite chuckles came from his parents.

Rico groaned. "That isn't very funny, Diego."

Diego shrugged. "I like jokes that make people groan. Puns are my favorite!"

When they finally reached the checkpoint, Papi showed their passports to the border patrol and answered some questions about their trip to Mexico. Who did they visit? How long had they been there? Where were they going now? Were they bringing anything back with them?

Diego held his breath. Would they have to unload all of the things from the van so they could be checked over? He released his breath as the border patrol waved the family on, satisfied with Papi's answers.

"Mami, we're in *Estados Unidos* now. Can I have the glasses?" Diego begged impatiently. "I need the box of animals that Don Toño gave us too. Do you have that?"

Mami reached under her seat and pulled out the shoebox. She looked back at her children, who were watching her with big eyes. "Yes, now is a good time. Thank you for your patience. I think the best idea is to wait to put on your glasses until you have the animal in your hand. What animal do you want?" she asked Diego.

"The owl!" he declared. "I can't wait to see what it's like to fly."

Rico leaned forward from his seat at the back of the van. "No, I want the owl!" he shouted. "Why should Diego get to pick?"

"Fine!" agreed Diego quickly. "I don't want to waste any more time. You can be the owl, and I'll be… the polar bear! Let's go, Mami!"

"Por favor," Mami reminded him as she passed the small stone polar bear to Diego, along with the owl for Rico. "Thank you for being a peacemaker, Diego."

"Sure," said Diego, painting a smile on his face. "I just want to go back to the Arctic!"

"Me *foca!*" declared Araceli, craning her neck to see the box on Mami's lap. "Where it go?"

"Can we have the glasses now, Mami?" interrupted Rico from the back.

"Slow down, kids," said Mami as she reached into the box and passed Araceli the baby harp seal. "I'm moving as fast as I can." She looked at her kids, who stared eagerly back at her with their hands outstretched. "When you put on the glasses, you'll be whisked back to the Arctic in the form of the animal you're holding. Are you ready?"
"Yes!" shouted the three Martinez kids in unison.

"Are you going to watch out for Araceli?" continued Mami.

"Yes!" they chorused.

"And if you need to come back, just take off your glasses, OK?" Mami reminded them.

"We know, Mami!" assured Diego. "Come on! *Por favor,*" he added, seeing his father glancing at him in the rear-view window as he drove.

"Thank you, Diego, for using your polite words," said Mami. She passed the kids their sunglasses. "Have fun!"

The kids cheered. After days of waiting, they would finally be going back to the Arctic. Clutching their stone statues, the Martinez kids quickly lifted their sunglasses up to their faces. "Woooooah!" they yelled excitedly as the van spun and a blast of cold air hit them.

Chapter 9
Back to the Arctic

As his eyes adjusted to the light again, Diego looked down to see shaggy white paws adorned by sharp black claws. Diego began to walk, working to coordinate his legs as he moved his enormous body forward on all fours. He was a polar bear! This was really happening! He let out a growl of excitement.

"Wow!" came Rico's voice from beside him.

Diego looked over to his right, and the sight took his breath away. A majestic snowy owl stood with his wings unfurled. Small gray spots speckled the white feathers. In the center of his round face was a tiny black beak set between two golden eyes.

"Wow, Rico! You look so *chido!*" marveled Diego.

"You look pretty amazing as a polar bear too!" admitted Rico, looking over Diego's enormous body covered in shaggy cream-colored fur. "I didn't realize how much bigger you would be than me."

A shrill sound by Diego's paws startled him. He jerked his head down to see where it had come from. A tiny white harp seal, who he recognized as Araceli, screamed in terror as she looked up at Diego looming over her. "Go 'way, bear! No eat me!" she cried, burying her furry head with her flipper.

"It's OK, Araceli. It's only Diego, not a real bear," Rico assured her. "Don't step on her!" he shouted up at the polar bear.

"Huh?" she asked, raising her head to look from the polar bear to the owl in confusion. "You Rico? And he Diego?"

"Yeah, it's me," assured Diego, carefully sidestepping his husky body away from his siblings to avoid accidentally hurting them. "I didn't mean to scare you!"

"You know, in real life you would be her predator," observed Rico wisely, speaking quietly so Araceli wouldn't hear him.

"I'm not going to hurt her," protested Diego. "She's my little sister! It's my job to protect her."

"I was hoping you'd say that!" exclaimed Rico quickly. "Would you mind watching Araceli while I go for a loop around?" Without waiting for a response, the owl prepared to fly away.

He paused for a moment, feeling the wind rustle his feathers. "How DO I fly?" he wondered. He began to flap his wings furiously. Instead of rising into the air as he expected, Rico flopped backward onto the ground. "I guess I'll have to practice," he concluded, feeling somewhat embarrassed as he picked himself up and shook the snow from his feathers.

Diego and Araceli stood with their mouths wide open as Rico flapped his wings once again, a bit more slowly. This time, he rose up and began to fly away clumsily, ducking and dipping as his body moved up into the air. "Look at me! I'm flying! I bet you wish you could fly too! See you later, lazybones!" he called as his feathered body moved crazily across the frigid blue sky and out of sight of his siblings.

"Wooow!" Diego watched his brother fly away. "I wish I could fly too!" He looked down at the little white seal flopped next to him. She was rolling around and giggling, enjoying her  roly-poly form. "Why do I always get stuck taking care of my baby sister?" he mumbled.

Then Diego remembered where he was. He was on a trademark Don Toño adventure in the Arctic, and he was a POLAR BEAR! He decided to take advantage of this opportunity.

"Come on, Araceli," he said. "Let's play hide-and-seek tag. I'll count and you hide, OK?" He looked down, expecting his sister to run away.

Instead, the little seal began to inch forward like a caterpillar, pushing herself ahead slowly with her little flippers. She flopped back down to the snowy ground. "This too hard!" she complained. "You carry me." She flipped onto her back and held her flippers up toward Diego.

Diego gave a frustrated sigh as he lowered his body to the snow so his sister could climb up onto his back. "Let's go, Araceli," he said. He raised his massive body with the fuzzy white seal balancing on his back. "Can you hang on?"

"You go slow. Me no want fall," she insisted, doing her best to clutch onto her brother's back.

Diego began to slowly plod forward. Araceli, perched on Diego's wide back, snuggled into his fur as if it were a cozy blanket. Naptime had arrived. Knowing she was safe with her big brother, her eyes began to close. The tiny harp seal drifted to sleep with the gentle movement of her brother's lumbering steps.

Diego grumbled to himself. This was not anything like he had expected. How was he going to have an adventure in the Arctic with his little sister riding on his back?

As soon as Diego heard a gentle snore from the tiny seal pup, he stopped next to a soft-looking snowbank. Tipping his body carefully, he slid Araceli off his back into a cozy nest. Her eyes remained closed and a small smile played across her puppylike face.

"She should be OK there for a while," Diego said to himself, ignoring the twinge of guilt that he felt. "Now I can go and find a REAL adventure." The polar bear plodded ahead, leaving the baby harp seal nestled in the snow, fast asleep.

Chapter 10
Hide-and-Seek

Diego trudged in the direction of the treeline, where a few prickly pine trees jutted out of the snow to the south. As he walked, he began talking to himself. "I wonder what polar bears do for fun? I would rather be flying right now."

"Polar bears don't fly! That's so silly!" came a voice from nearby. Suddenly two young polar bears about his size popped up from behind a snowbank. "We play!" The smaller of the two bears giggled in a friendly voice and walked up to Diego with a curious expression on her furry white face.

"Who are you?" asked Diego shyly, looking at the bears. Usually it was Rico who met new friends first.

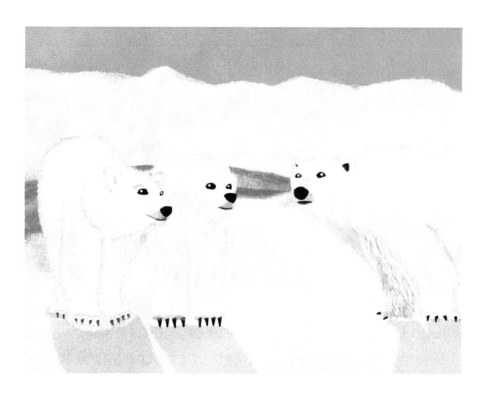

The bigger bear looked at Diego, his grin revealing sharp teeth in what Diego imagined was a friendly expression. "I'm Nanook and this is my sister Nuka," the bear explained, gesturing with his snout toward the other bear.

"Hi," Diego greeted them, waving his paw in the air. "I've never heard those names before. What do they mean?"

"*Nanook* means 'polar bear' in the Inuit language. They're the humans who live around here. And *Nuka* means 'little sister,'" replied Nanook.

"I like it!" said Diego, growing more confident. "My name is Diego. It's Spanish, but I don't know what it means. My neighbor Don Toño would be able to tell you. He's so smart! He's the reason I'm here today!"

"Huh?" questioned Nuka, scrunching up her black polar bear nose. "What do you mean?"

"Well," said Diego thoughtfully. "It's hard to explain. Let's just say I'm not from around here. But it's so *chido* to be a polar bear!"

Nuka bounced up and down on her stocky back legs. "Nanook, can we show Diego around? He's sooo nice."

Nanook looked at Nuka. "I don't know. You're so little. Are you sure you can keep up with us?"

Nuka started to pout.

Diego looked from one bear cub to the other. "Come on, we can all play together. Who wants to play hide-and-seek? I'll count to 20 and you both hide!"

"Sure! We love hide-and-seek! Our super sense of smell makes the game extra exciting!" explained Nanook. "We can catch a whiff of other animals 20 miles away, and even smell a seal three feet under the ice!"

"That's crazy!" marveled Diego, sniffing to pick up the mix of scents blowing in the Arctic breeze. He was amazed to realize that his instincts were working, and he was able to identify the distinct fishy smell of the two friendly polar bears standing in front of him. "The sense of smell is definitely working, Don Toño!" he spoke into the air.

The three young bears headed off together to play their game. As he walked toward the treeline with Nanook and Nuka, Diego forgot that he had left Araceli peacefully snuggled in her snowy bed.

"Do you want to know how to count to twenty in Spanish? Let me teach you!" said Diego to Nanook. *"Uno, dos, tres, cuatro, cinco…"* he began counting. He looked up to see his new friends watching him. "Go on, you have to go hide!"

They laughed and took off in different directions.

"...*Diecinueve, veinte!*" finished Diego. "Ready or not, here I come!"

Diego opened his eyes and scanned the scene surrounding him. The polar bears' white coats made it almost impossible to spot them against the snow. "Wow, camouflage is amazing!" he said to himself. Then his nose tickled him and he knew exactly where one of his friends was hiding. "Woah! This is too easy!" He checked behind a snowdrift and found Nanook hiding there. "I see you!"

Nanook laughed. "That reminds me of a joke I know. What did one polar bear say to the other during hide-and-seek?"

"I give up!" responded Diego.

"ICY you! Get it? I-see-you?" Nanook looked at Diego expectantly.

"Ba-dum-pum-CHING!" said Diego, imitating a drum rimshot. He laughed and looked at Nanook. "I've got one! Where do polar bears keep their money?"

He paused as Nanook shook his head. "In a snowbank!"

Diego finished. He and Nanook laughed and playfully wrestled, enjoying their new friendship.

"Hey, I know a really great place to play hide-and-seek!" said Nanook suddenly. "There's an abandoned weather station nearby where all the cubs go to play. You're going to think this is so cool... or what was that word you used? *Chido.*"

Diego followed Nanook as they traipsed through the drifts to a broken-down, faded wooden building the size of a small cabin. Nanook pushed the door open with his nose and stepped into the building. "Isn't this a cool hideout?"

Diego's eyes adjusted as he stepped out of the direct sunlight. The inside of the building looked like no people had been there for a long time. The wooden floor had slats missing, and long dead grass poked up from the ground below. Up above, rays of sharp Arctic sunlight shone through the holes in the rotting boards of the roof. The glass in the windows had been broken, allowing the wind to blow drifted snow in a dance around the cabin. In the corner on a worn table sat an old-fashioned, rusty radio.

"Woooah!" said Diego. "This IS *chido!*" He walked over to the radio and rose up on his hind legs to prop his paws on the table. "Roger, roger, I hear you loud and clear," he said in his best radio voice. He plopped back down and looked around to see where his friend had gone.

Nanook was standing at one of the broken windows, peering outside thoughtfully. "I like to stand here and watch what's going on in the neighborhood."

Diego stood next to Nanook and looked out at a few prickly pine trees scattered across the otherwise desolate landscape. "Wow," he commented, looking around. "It's so peaceful. It's like we're the last living things on earth. Being a polar bear is so much better than I thought it would be! I can't wait to tell my brother Rico about playing with you and Nuka!"

Suddenly, a concerned look came over Nanook's face. "Oh no! Where did Nuka go?" he asked urgently. "I don't see her anywhere! My mom made me promise to keep an eye on my sister."

"I'll help you find her!" offered Diego. The bear cubs plodded as quickly as they could through the open

door of the abandoned cabin and moved through the snowbanks, calling, "Nuka!" and sniffing with their black noses.

A second later, a furry white head popped out from behind a snowdrift. "I'm right here!" she called in a singsong voice. "You couldn't find me! I won the game! Why did you take so long?"

Nanook ran over and gave his sister a big bear hug. "I was worried I had lost you, Nuka! I'm so glad you're here."

At that moment, Diego got a sinking feeling that traveled all the way down to the pit of his belly. Araceli. Where was Araceli? His large head swung from side to side and his world began to spin as he entered into a panic.

"My sister! I lost my sister!" he said urgently to Nanook and Nuka.

The bears looked at him strangely. "I didn't know you had a sister. Where is she?"

"That's what I don't know!" said Diego, his eyes

welling up with tears. "I left her behind in a snowbank because I wanted to play."

"But I didn't see any other polar bears with you," said Nuka to Diego. "I would have liked to play with a girl polar bear."

Diego shook his head. "She's not a polar bear. She's... a baby harp seal."

"Huh?!" Nanook and Nuka looked at him like he was crazy. "I don't know why you would call a seal your sister. Wouldn't a seal be a snack?" questioned Nanook.

"No!" shouted Diego frantically. "I didn't tell you the truth! It's a long story, but I need to find her now! I can't let anything happen to her. What if a polar bear tries to eat her?!" He saw confusion on the faces of his new friends. Tears began to flow down his face.

"I said I would protect her. Why did I forget?" A gust of wind kicked up and icy crystals began to swirl around him. He suddenly felt very cold and alone. "Where is Araceli? What am I going to do?"

Chapter 11
Flying Lessons

Rico the snowy owl flapped his white and gray feathered wings as hard as he could, rising clumsily into the air with jagged movements. He still felt like he didn't know what he was doing.

"Look at me! I'm flying! I bet you wish you could fly too! See you later, lazybones!" His words echoed in his ears as he remembered watching Diego and Araceli draw farther away on the ice below. He felt a brief flash of guilt, but quickly pushed it away.

A forceful gust of Arctic wind caught Rico by surprise. He lost his rhythm and began to careen downward, hitting the ground. "That one hurt," he mumbled to himself, glancing around to see if

anyone had seen his crash-landing.

Just then, another snowy owl swooped down gracefully and landed next to Rico. "What's going on? Are you having a hard time flying today?" he asked.

Rico looked ashamed and glanced down at his black talons. "I'm just learning," he mumbled.

"Oh." The owl looked at him with a puzzled look in his almond-shaped yellow eyes. "I guess we all have to learn at some time." He reached out his wing to pat Rico on the back. "Would you like some help?"

Rico hesitated. "I don't know... it isn't really going so well. What if somebody laughs at me?"

The other owl chuckled. "You should have seen me when I was learning to fly. I lost control and crashed right in front of my big brother. He made so much fun of me after that. He called me Ookpik the Oops."

"Ookpik?" questioned Rico.

"Yeah, that's my name. Don't laugh. It means 'snowy owl' in Inuit," answered Ookpik.

"I'm not laughing. I like your name," said Rico kindly. "I'm sorry your brother made fun of you. I tease my little brother sometimes. I know he doesn't like it."

Ookpik nodded as if he understood. "So, what's your name?"

"I'm Rico. It means 'rich' in Spanish... or 'delicious.'"

"Nobody's going to eat you when you're a snowy owl! You're at the top of the food chain!" exclaimed Ookpik. "We get to eat all the little animals like lemmings and fish. Anyway, who wants to have some flying lessons?"

"I do!" exclaimed Rico. He flapped his downy wings up and down frantically, raising himself into the air for a moment before falling on his back on the snow. "I don't know why that keeps happening," he said in a dejected voice. "I'm the WORST flyer ever."

Rico glanced over at Ookpik, surprised to see his friend had his beak clenched together. Ookpik caught Rico's eye, and after a moment both owls began to hoot with laughter. "Sorry about that," Ookpik apologized when they quieted down.

"It WAS pretty funny," agreed Rico, now more relaxed. "Can you tell me what I'm doing wrong?"

"Well, to start, you don't need to flap so hard. It's all about the glide," said Ookpik smoothly. "Spread your wings, give a few strong flaps, and then keep them spread out wide." He showed Rico his five-foot wingspan.

Rico extended his wings and made a small leap. He flapped deliberately and kept his wings outstretched. His feathered body rose off the ground and began to glide through the air a few feet off the ground.

"It worked! I'm flying!" he called, realizing he could rotate his head all the way backward to see his friend behind him. "Come on, Ookpik!"

Rico quickly learned that looking backward while flying was probably not the wisest idea. His moment of triumph ended abruptly as he crashed into a prickly pine tree.

"Ouch!" he uttered as his body once again fell into a snowdrift. "I think my instincts are broken this time, Don Toño!" he called into the Arctic wind in a discouraged voice.

Ookpik flew to Rico with ease and landed on the

ground. "Whoooo are you talking to?" he hooted.

Rico laughed and temporarily forgot the pain he was in. He shook the snow off his wings and stood up. "That's funny! My brother and I love puns. Um... here's one! Knock, knock."

Ookpik knew just how to respond. "Whooooo's there?" he hooted.

"Owl."

"Owl whoooooo?"

"OWL come in now!" finished Rico triumphantly. "Get it? I'LL come in now?"

Ookpik looked at him seriously for a moment. "That wasn't very funny," he said, staring at him intently with his golden eyes. Then a cackle exited from his curved beak. "Just kidding. That was HOOOmerous!"

Rico groaned. "Humorous? Like funny? These puns keep getting worse." He laughed along with his friend. Then he remembered he was discouraged. "Maybe I should give up on flying and we can just tell jokes til it's time for me to go."

Ookpik stopped laughing. "Let's give it one more try, little buddy. You're so close! I can feel it. This time you're going to get it!"

"I'm just not used to having to try so hard," confessed Rico. "Usually I'm the best at everything in my family since I'm the oldest."

Ookpik nodded. "Maybe this is how your little brother feels when he's trying to keep up with you. It's not fun to always be in your older brother's shadow."

Rico nodded. "He and my sister always want to do everything I do. It gets annoying sometimes. Being the oldest is tough," he reflected.

"That's true, but being the younger owlet isn't always easy either," said Ookpik wisely. "Now, about those flying lessons… are you ready to try again?"

Rico looked at the white ground around him, then up at the blue Arctic sky. Taking a deep breath, he turned to his friend. "Let's do it!"

Chapter 12
Up in the Air

"Here, follow me!" Ookpik gave a small hop, flapped his wings a few times, then took off gliding in the air to a tree branch a few yards away. "Come on, Rico!" he encouraged. "Fly, Rico, fly! Spread your wings! You can DO it! "

"Sí, se puede!" Rico repeated to himself. He hopped, flapped, and spread his wings, soaring a few feet off the ground. Ookpik launched into the air from the branch and began to fly with him. Flapping his strong wings slowly and steadily, Rico gained altitude. "It's working! Whoo hoooo!" he hooted happily. "This feels amazing!" The two owls flew side-by-side, enjoying the feeling of the wind under their wide wings.

"You can see everything from here," Rico observed as he flew.

"We do have excellent vision," agreed Ookpik. "Look, there's a lemming down on the ground. Are you hungry?"

"Um, I don't think I'm in the mood for a lemming right now…" began Rico, remembering his earlier adventure in the Arctic. "Do you know where we could find a *quesadilla?*"

"A what?" questioned Ookpik.

"Nevermind," decided Rico. He concentrated on flying and made a swoop in the air. "This is getting easier, Ookpik! I can't believe I know how to fly now! Diego and Araceli are going to be so jealous!"

Ookpik looked over at him as they flew. "Why don't you want the younger owlets to fly too? You could fly together. Their success wouldn't make your success any less impressive."

Rico stayed silent as he passed through an especially puffy white cloud. "You're right, Ookpik," he sighed.

"I really do love my brother and sister, even though we argue sometimes. I could be more encouraging to them. You've shown me that it means a lot to have somebody believe in you."

His keen eyes focused on a scene on the snowy ground ahead of him. A polar bear was standing on his hind legs, waving his front paws in the air. Could that be Diego? Suddenly Rico remembered the way he had left his siblings behind. "Hey, Ookpik, can we go that direction? I think I'm ready to be done."

Ookpik looked disappointed. "We're just getting going!" he complained, but he began to glide to a lower altitude.

Rico followed, letting himself soar gently to a pine tree branch. "I should probably say goodbye for now," he said to Ookpik. "I need to get back to my family. Thanks for the flying lessons. I'm really glad you got me to stick with it."

The other owl followed Rico's gaze to see what he was looking at. "Why is that polar bear waving its paws around like that? The animals are acting strange around here today." He shrugged with a flap of his wings, then turned to Rico. "Thanks, little buddy! Hope to see you around here again soon. You can join the frequent flyers club with me anytime!" He launched himself into the air and gracefully soared away.

Rico glided down closer to the young polar bear waving at him. "Diego, is that you?" he called happily. "Look, I learned how to fly!" As he flew closer, his sharp eyes noticed a teardrop glistening on the bear's face. He landed gracefully next to his brother. "Diego, what's wrong?" he asked.

Diego looked at Rico with a terrified look in his eyes. "It's Araceli!" he said breathlessly. "She's missing!"

Chapter 13
The Missing Seal

"What do you mean, she's missing?" Rico's golden eyes glinted angrily. "Didn't you say you would watch her while I was gone?"

"No, YOU said I had to watch her, then you just took off. It isn't fair that I didn't get to be the owl AND I had to drag around a little seal with me." Diego bared his teeth in anger, then his expression softened as he looked at Rico. "I really messed up, didn't I?"

Rico was hit with a pang of guilt. "It's my fault too. It really wasn't fair of me, was it? I shouldn't have dumped the responsibility on you, and now our little sister might be in trouble. We have to find her!"

"Do you want to search this way and I'll look over there?" questioned Diego, looking at his older brother for guidance.

"No," decided Rico firmly. "We need to work together on this. I can fly up high and scan the area to see if I can find her. These owl eyes are super sharp! Don Toño really did a good job with the senses!"

"Good idea," agreed Diego. "I discovered polar bears have an amazing sense of smell, so that will help me to search down here on the ground."

"Perfect!" agreed Rico. "Can you catch a whiff of the direction we should go?"

Diego lifted his black muzzle in the air and drew in a deep breath of icy Arctic air. As he did, it was as if a switch had been turned on. A medley of different scents filled his nose, bringing to mind images of fish, bears, foxes, rabbits, and seals. "Woah, I can smell everything! How will I ever know which one is her?"

"Concentrate, Diego!" encouraged Rico. "Think

about what Araceli smelled like when she was a seal. Can you remember? We can't do this without you! You're the super-sniffer!"

Diego closed his eyes and took another deep breath. He thought about his little sister: her snow-white fur and cuddly little body; and her round black eyes and little black nose with adorable whiskers making her look like a puppy. Suddenly, her scent came to him. "I smell her!" he exclaimed to Rico. Rotating his head, he concentrated on the direction the scent was the strongest. "I think she's that way!" he said hopefully, gesturing with his snout.

Rico had been silently observing his little brother. "Great job, Diego!" he congratulated the polar bear.

"OK, it's my turn now. I'm going to see if I can spot her. I'll be right back!" Pushing himself upward with his taloned feet, the majestic snowy owl launched into the air. Flapping his strong wings, he took off, soaring through the air like an old pro.

Rico arrived at flying altitude, scanning the area in the direction that Diego had indicated. As he flew, his eyes locked in on a variety of creatures. Beautiful white foxes and rabbits, who would have been indistinguishable to his human eyes against the snowy background, showed up as if a telescope lens were being focused in on them.

Rico smiled to himself as he watched a family of lemmings scurry across the snow, remembering his earlier adventure with his siblings. It really HAD been fun working together with them and letting each lemming have their moment to shine as they solved the mystery of the hidden clue. His time with Ookpik had made him think that maybe being the oldest wasn't the most important thing, after all.

Suddenly, Rico's eyes zeroed in on a movement below him. A white ball of fur was rolling around in the snow. His heart began to beat quickly. It was

Araceli! Next to her, a wrinkled brown walrus with long tusks sat, watching the baby harp seal play.

Swooping back around, he flew to where Diego was waiting. "I found her! She's OK!" he informed his brother happily. "You were right about the direction."

"Yay!" cheered Diego joyfully, standing up on his back paws to do a polar bear dance in the snow. "Let's go!" He dropped down on all fours and began to walk, with Rico flying in slow circles above him.

"Uh, there's one more thing I didn't tell you," confessed Rico. "Don Toño is there with her. I have a feeling he's not going to be happy that we just left her by herself."

"Oh no!" worried Diego. "He's going to tell Mami and Papi that I left Araceli alone. I'm going to be in so much trouble!"

"WE are going to be in trouble together," assured Rico. "She was OUR responsibility. We'll tell them the truth. I'm just glad that we found her." He paused for a moment, thinking about everything

that had happened since they'd arrived in the Arctic. "We really DO make a good team, don't we?"

"Yeah, we really do," agreed Diego, craning his neck to look at the owl above him. "She's right ahead; I can smell her!" he added expertly.

The pair reached the snowy expanse where Don Toño was sitting with Araceli. As they got closer, they could hear the little seal singing a familiar song at the top of her lungs. Don Toño chuckled and clapped his flippers together when she finished her performance.

"Yay, Araceli!" the brothers cheered as they approached. "We missed you so much!"

"Diego! Rico! You back!" the white seal exclaimed with a look of joy on her adorable face. Then the expression changed to confusion. "Where you go?"

Don Toño looked over his spiky whiskers at the owl and the polar bear. "Yes, *chamacos,* where DID you go? Didn't you promise your parents you would take care of your sister?"

"Sorry, Araceli," confessed Diego sadly, bringing his big head down to look her in the eyes. "I shouldn't have left you."

Araceli smiled and gave Diego's giant paw a pat with her fuzzy flipper. "It OK," she said, forgiving him quickly.

"We will take whatever punishment Mami and Papi give us," added Rico bravely. "We know we were wrong. We deserve to have our tablets taken away from us for the rest of the drive back to Minnesota."

"Yeah!" added Diego. "And listen to boring old-people music!"

Don Toño hid a grin on his tusked mouth and looked at the boys thoughtfully. "I'll leave that up to your parents," he decided. "It sounds like you've learned your lesson, am I right?"

"Yes!" affirmed Diego. "We learned that we love our sister SO much and never want anything to happen to her… and that we are able to do so much more if we work together instead of fighting with each other."

"Yeah," agreed Rico. "And I learned that I don't always need to have my way because I'm the oldest." He looked at Diego. "You should be the owl next time."

Diego's polar bear face frowned. "I don't think I could fly like you do. I'm too little."

Rico paused for a moment. It would be pretty

special to be the only Martinez kid who knew how to fly. Then he remembered Ookpik's encouragement. "That's not true, Diego. I can teach you. You'll be able to do it!"

"Me fly too!" declared Araceli with determination. "Me big *foca.*"

Don Toño chuckled. "You're not going to fly too far in that little harp seal body, *chiquita,*" he said affectionately. "The next time you kids come to the Arctic, maybe you can all be owls and fly together."

"Yeah, we should come back soon," agreed Diego. "But not today. I'm hungry! I think it's time to go back to… where are we in real life?"

"Your family is making their way up through Texas," said Don Toño. "I spoke to your mami by phone a little while ago and she wants you kids to take a break soon."

"It's weird to think that we're still sitting in the van, and you're back in Minnesota. This feels SO real!" pondered Rico.
"Yeah!" agreed Diego. "How do we go back again,

Don Toño?"

"You need to take off your glasses. Reach up and touch your face and they will come off, even though you can't see them right now," instructed Don Toño. "OK, *chamacos?*"

"*Muchas gracias,* Don Toño," the siblings thanked him.

"On the count of three," coached the walrus.

"*¡Uno, dos, tres!*" they all counted together.

Chapter 14
Reunited

Diego pawed his face and was surprised to feel his world start to spin. Suddenly, he was strapped into his seat in the van. Sitting next to him, and a little girl once again, Araceli was blinking her eyes like she had just woken up from a deep sleep. Behind him, Rico rubbed his eyes with his hands.

"Welcome back to real life, *hijos,*" came the voice of Papi from the driver's seat. "I was beginning to wonder if you were going to stay in the Arctic forever."

"No, Papi," assured Diego. "It's fun to have adventures, but I love our family too much. I would miss you and Mami."

"Maybe we need to come along next time," suggested Mami. "Do you think Don Toño can make some adult-sized glasses for Papi and me?"

"Yay! We be *focas!*" exclaimed Araceli.

"Being a polar bear was so *chido!*" added Diego. "I made the nicest friends all by myself, and they took me to see an old weather station! I'm glad I was a polar bear!"

"Flying was amazing!" Rico said. "If you come with us next time, you should be owls!"

"Wow, you kids have a lot to share with us," observed Mami as all three kids began to chatter at once about their experiences. "What do you say we stop for lunch and you can each share about your adventure in the Arctic? What sounds good to eat?"

"Anything but lemmings!" exclaimed Rico, and the family laughed.

Just then Mami's phone buzzed and she paused to read it. She turned around again. "So, boys, how did things go with Araceli?"

"Well," began Diego quietly, his eyes welling up with tears. "I didn't take care of her like I promised I would. I'm SO sorry!"

"And I left her behind too!" confessed Rico. "I know there is going to be a consequence."

Papi and Mami glanced at each other in the front seats, communicating silently.

Mami turned back around and looked her sons in the eyes. "Don Toño texted me about how you worked together to find her. We trust you have learned a lesson. This may have been virtual reality, but it is still important to take care of her."

"That's right!" said Diego adamantly. "I will NEVER let anything bad happen to my little sister. I love her SO much!"

Araceli smiled happily. "Love you!" she shouted, blowing kisses to her brothers.

"By the way, Araceli," Rico questioned. "What did you do while we were off exploring?"

"No sé," she shrugged, picking up a princess book and holding it in front of her face.

The boys exchanged a look. "I bet she just slept the whole time until Don Toño found her," decided Rico.

"I guess we'll never know..." agreed Diego, shrugging his shoulders.

Sitting in her carseat and hiding behind her book, Araceli hid a smile.

As the van continued up the highway and back to the cold Minnesota winter, the Martinez family had warm hearts. It had been an incredible trip to Mexico by way of the Arctic, and they were so thankful to be together.

Epilogue
Araceli's Story

Araceli awoke from her nap to someone gently nudging her. She kept her eyes closed and tried to snuggle under her warm blanket to fall back asleep. "Me sleep more, Mami," she said drowsily, wishing she could return to her dream where she was a cute little baby seal.

The nudging continued, and she heard a voice that did not belong to Mami. "Hello, baby seal! What are you doing here?"

Araceli began to open her eyes and had to squint as the bright sunlight entered through the slits. She was surprised to see she was not in her bedroom, and definitely not snuggled under her covers on her

bed. She was covered in a light blanket of snow with just her little black nose peeking out. "Yay! Me foca!" She shook her body to free herself from the loose powder and looked at the source of the voice.

There, flopped next to her, was a seal that was quite a bit bigger than she was. Rather than white like Araceli's, this seal's coat was a gray color with black spots. The seal smiled at her. "You're just a baby, aren't you? You've still got your downy lanugo coat."

Araceli looked defiantly at the bigger seal. "Me no baby! Me big! Me Araceli!"
"Oh, excuse me," the seal giggled and began to

speak quickly. "Good to meet you, big Araceli. My name is Sakari. It means 'sweet'! You're just a little seal. Do you need help? Where are your parents?"

Araceli stared at Sakari as the older seal chattered on. She reached up and put her flipper over the bigger seal's whiskered mouth, causing Sakari to stop speaking. "Me like you. You my *amiga?*" Araceli asked.

"What's an *amiga?*" asked Sakari. "I don't think I speak that language."

"Look," explained Araceli firmly. "We play. OK?" She rolled over on her back and giggled, waggling her flippers in the air and flopping her tail up and down on the ice. "You. Me. Princess *focas!*"

"I get it!" shouted Sakari. "You want to be friends. Of course!" She propped herself up on her flippers and looked at the little white seal. "Hey, Araceli, it's pretty hard for seals like us to move on land. Do you want to go swimming? I can teach you!"

Araceli looked at her older friend excitedly. "We go beach?" she asked, looking around for a sandy shore like the Minnesota lakes her family liked to visit in the summer.

"What's a beach? We go in through the hole in the ice over there," answered Sakari, gesturing with her flipper. She pulled herself forward until she came to the edge of the ice. "I'm getting to be a pretty good swimmer. They call me a 'beater' sometimes because I'm still a little bit klutzy and beat my tail around in the water, but I'm getting better. Come on!"

Araceli looked at the hole in the ice and her little mind had a moment of clarity. She didn't know how to swim. "Me scared. No want to."

"But the sea unicorns are down there swimming around! Don't you want to go see a narwhal? They're so exciting and magical!" exclaimed Sakari.

"U-corns?" Araceli's whiskers, sticking out from her little black nose, twitched excitedly. She had a unicorn stuffy at home. Could there really be unicorns that swim in the water? She had to see for herself.

Sakari pulled herself to the hole in the ice with her

flippers. "Look! I think I see one right now! Come on, princess seal! I'll teach you!" encouraged Sakari, flopping into the water with a splash.

Araceli looked down at her new friend in the water. "Me brave *foca,*" she assured herself. She pushed herself into the icy water.

"Yay! Now you swim like this," instructed Sakari, clumsily beating her flippers and tail in the water to demonstrate.
The older seal looked over at Araceli and saw that

she was frantically thrashing and starting to sink in the water. Araceli tried to cry but her mouth filled up with ice water.

"Oh no! You need to swim, little seal!" Suddenly Sakari glanced under the water and screamed: "Gotta go!" She ducked her gray head and quickly swam away.

At that moment, a huge walrus swam up under Araceli, pushing her out of the water and onto the ice with his whiskered snout. The walrus then jabbed his long yellowish tusks into the ice to heft his own enormous body out of the water. The two dripping animals rested on the ice. Araceli lay there in silence, stunned for a minute, then let out an ear-splitting wail.

"Todo bien, chiquita. You're OK," assured the familiar voice of Don Toño. Araceli shivered and continued to cry as Don Toño comforted her gently. He stroked her small head with his flipper. "What were you doing in the water? You aren't ready to swim yet. Baby harp seals aren't even waterproof until they get bigger. Where are your *hermanos?"*
Araceli blinked away her tears. *"No sé,"* she

answered. Looking up at Don Toño, she relaxed. She knew she was safe now. "You my *amigo,*" she said happily, leaning her fuzzy white face forward to give him a kiss on his flipper.

The little seal attempted a somersault, then enthusiastically began to sing one of her favorite songs about the snow.

Don Toño chuckled to himself as he listened to

Araceli's impromptu concert. "These *chamacos* keep me young," he thought affectionately. "I can't wait to plan their next adventure!"

The Piñata Song

Dale, dale, dale, no pierdas el tino,
Porque si lo pierdes, pierdes el camino.
Ya le diste una, ya le diste dos,
¡Ya le diste tres y tu tiempo se acabó!

Go, go, go! Don't lose your aim,
Because if you miss, you'll lose your way.
Now you hit it once, now you hit it twice,
Now you hit it three times and your time is up!

Tita's Atole de Avena
(Hot Oatmeal Drink)

Ingredients:
4 cups of water

½ cup sugar

2 cinnamon sticks

1 can of evaporated milk (12 oz)

1 cup oatmeal

1 pinch of salt

Note: Tita reminds you to ask an adult for help when working with a hot stove.

Instructions:
1. Boil 4 cups of water with ½ cup sugar and 2 sticks of cinnamon.
2. When the water begins to boil, stir in 1 can of evaporated milk.
3. When it returns to a boil, stir in 1 cup of oatmeal.
4. Let it cook on low heat for 10 minutes, stirring occasionally.
5. Add a pinch of salt.
6. Serve the *atole* in mugs and enjoy it hot!

A Note from Minda Gomez

Yes, that's me! Did you know that the Martinez family is based on my own family?

I hope you enjoyed reading about Rico, Diego, and Araceli's adventures in the Arctic! Wouldn't you like to have a neighbor like Don Toño and get to go on wild animal adventures? I know I would!

If you enjoyed the story, please consider asking your parents to leave a review online so that other readers can also discover the books. Thank you!

Contact Me

Website: **www.mindagomez.com**
Email: **martinezkidsadventures@gmail.com**
Instagram/Facebook: **@martinezkidsadventures**
YouTube: Martinez Kids Adventures

I would love to hear any suggestions you have for future Martinez Kids Adventures. What animals would you like to read about in the next book? What lessons do they need to learn? Let me know in an email or on social media. It would make my day to hear from you!

Check out my website to sign up for my newsletter, and for bonus material like discussion questions, Spanish pronunciations, videos, and my store.

If you enjoyed this book, make sure you check out Book 1: *The Secret Door*, also available in Spanish!

About the Author

Minda Gomez lives in Minnesota with her husband and three spunky bilingual kids. Their family has created their own brand of "Mexigringo" as they blend their Papi's Mexican culture with their Mami's Minnesotan culture.

Minda is a teacher of English Learners at a local elementary school. She has taught second grade in Mexico and volunteered as an English teacher in Guatemala, Thailand, and Mexico.

Minda is passionate about teaching children and families to be proud of their bilingual superpowers. She is hopeful that her readers will identify with the Martinez family, and remember that speaking more than one language is one of the many things that can make a kid special.

CPSIA information can be obtained
at www.ICGtesting.com
Printed in the USA
BVHW010408150722
642106BV00001B/9